MW01156588

THE AZURES

THE AZURES

Alex Begandy

Library of Congress Control Number:		2021922589
ISBN:	Hardcover	978-1-6641-9855-5
	Softcover	978-1-6641-9854-8
	eBook	978-1-6641-9853-1

Print information available on the last page.

Rev. date: 11/05/2021

To order additional copies of this book, contact:
Xlibris
844-714-8691
www.Xlibris.com
Orders@Xlibris.com
837288

CHAPTER 1

On a beach in Hawaii, the famous boxer Stewie "the hothead" Sin enjoys his time off after defending his title. As he stood there watching the waves crash into the shore. "The water can be a peaceful thing," he said smiling. "I should bring my sister here someday."

Then suddenly the ground started shaking, as people began running. He stood there looking around at everyone running, "Excuse me, miss….. Sir? Hey sir?" He was trying to get someone as a long blue-haired lady bumped into him. "I'm sorry, Stewie," She apologized. "It's fine; what's going on?" Stewie asked as he looked at her.

She points to the volcano, "Mt. Beatle is going to erupt any second now, and…" her sentence was cut short from a blast from the volcano. "Oh no," She gasps as she sees the volcano erupting. "I left my hotel key on the table." She said. "I can't lose that again."

"Where did you leave it?" Stewie asked.

She looked at him in awe. "On the table over there." She replied, pointing to it. "But the lava is closing. You won't make it." As he faced the table, he looked back at her, "Watch me," he said as he started sprinting.

"He won't make it," she sighed as she hoped she was wrong. As soon as Stewie grabbed the card, he became dizzy, and his vision started getting blurred. A cloaked figure was close by watching. "What the…. My vision," he said as the lava has moved closer. "What's happening to my vision?" he said as he realized that the lava had gotten closer as he started running back.

The Blue-haired lady watched him as the lava was catching up with him. "He's almost here," she said worriedly. "But the lava," Flashes of the cloaked figure looking at him in front of him. "What's with my vision?" he said as he looked at the lava as he ran.

"Is it the lava that's affecting me?" he said as he looked back. "Catch!" he yelled as he threw the card over to the woman. When she caught her card, Stewie tripped over suddenly. "Oh no," the ladygaspedp as the lava covered Stewie. She started to run away as she knew that she couldn't help. After the lava hardened, a skeleton hand popped out. "I need to get out," he said, gasping.

He made a hole in the hardened lava, "Ow," he said, rubbing his neck. "Wait, how am I alive?" He continued as he looked at his body. "I'm a skeleton?"

A giant treasure chest appeared. As Stewie noticed, he walked to the chest and grabbed the note attached to it reading it. "You now have the power of an Azure. An Azure is an elemental god. Your element is fire and in the chest is your armor and weapon. There are three other Azures in the area. Find them and learn to control your powers." Stewie set the note down, put his lava armor on and his sword on his back. "I guess I have to find the other Azures," he said, "But where should I begin?"

Chapter 2

As the woman got to the safe place away from the lava, she passed out in front of a hotel where someone found her and brought her inside. After a few hours, she'd woke up not knowing where she was. "Wh-where am I?" she asked.

She got up and looked around as a front desk clerk appeared behind her. "You are at the Abby Hotel Ms, Luna. I found you outside and helped you in," he said. She jumps a bit, "The Abby hotel?" She asked as she looked around, "Must be a new hotel, I guess. Wait, what about the lava?"

"Don't worry, Luna, it appears to have stopped rather quickly," he replied as he turned on the news. "We have confirmed that the lava has stopped," the newscaster said as the news chopper flew overhead. "The police have not found ether Stewie "The hothead" Sin or Luna "Rainfall" Kitty and are currently still searching for them," she said.

She then looks up. "This just in, there seems to be a skeleton in lava armor on the beach, appearing to be looking for something."

Luna looked at the skeleton, realizing who it was. "Stewie!" she gasped.

"Wait, what? The clerk asked, "You mean that skeleton in Stewie?"

"Yes, that's him, I'm sure of it. I have to go and thank you for helping," Luna said as she raced out of the hotel and headed towards the beach. The clerk smiles, "come back anytime… Luna," he says as he looks back at the tv. "She's on her way, great one," he said, bowing.

Soon she arrived at the beach and started looking around. "Stewie! Stewie! Where are you?" she called out. As she continued to look around, a tentacle grabbed her legs from behind and pulled her into the water. "Aaah! Help," she yelled. As he heard Luna yelling, Stewie came running. "Let her go!" Stewie said as he launched towards the giant tentacle, but he was too late, and Luna was dragged into the ocean.

Stewie stood up, looking at the sea. "How am I going to save her?" he asked himself.

Meanwhile, in the water, Luna is struggling to escape when she hears a voice.

"Please stop squirming, Luna," he said, "I have summoned you here to give you the power of water."

He forms a giant air bubble around her. "I forget you humans need air," he said. As Lunagaspedp, "Wh-why didn't you come onto land? Also, who are you?" she asked. He walked into the bubble as he held up his hand, summoning a small light source that revealed his fishy features, and looked at Luna.

"Call me, Captain Jones, an elder god of sorts gave me this power of water centuries ago," he said,

"You will receive the same power and join three others on land." he continued as he placed his hand on her forehead. "This will only take a second."

Water swirls around Luna as she gasps.

After the water disputes, Luna was in a buccaneer suit with twin pistols and gills on the sides of her abdomen. Luna opens her eyes and looks down at herself wide-eyed. "I feel stronger now." She said as she spun her guns.

"This is only the beginning, Luna." Jones said, "With that done, my time is up."

Luna looked at him as he disappeared into the watery depths. "Thanks, I guess," she said as she looked around as the air bubble started filling up with water. "Guess I need to find the others, Shouldn't be hard to find... right?" she asked herself as she jumped out and landed close by to Stewie.

Stewie looks over at her. "Luna?" he questioned.

"Yes, it's me," she replied as she looked at him, smiling. "How do you feel, Luna?" Stewie asked. "Mhm, Oh, I'm fine, and you Stewie?" She replied,

"Still a bit confused with the whole thing, but I'll live, I think." Stewie said, "I see you have become the water, Azure."

"As you are fire," she continued. "We should make names for ourselves."

"How about Magma and Kira?" Stewie asked. "Sounds good. Should we see if we can find the others, Magma?" Kira asked. "Why not Kira?" Magma replied as they started walking. "Where should we start first?" Magma continued.

"With any luck, they will find us," Kira said.

CHAPTER 3

Meanwhile, Drew "headstrong" Jack worked out on his upper core on the other side of town. "99...100," He said as he dropped to the floor and took off the weights. As he warped a towel over his neck, a girl came running in. "Dad, Mt. Beatle has erupted." she started saying. "Now, a skeleton with lava armor and a female sea captain has appeared on the beach."

Drew walked up to her putting his hand on her shoulder. "Don't worry, I'm sure they're harmless," he said as the gym started shaking.

"What was that?" he asked. "Possible earthquake?" she replied as the ground split open, separating the two.

"Get to the safe house," Drew said, looking around. She looked at him, worried, "What about you?" she asked worriedly. "Don't worry about me, I'll find," He started to say when another shockwave hit. "Hurry, and get to the safe house. There's no time," He said, "I'll be there when I can."

She looked down "yes, father." she said as she left running. After she left, the ground split open under Drew, but he reacted fast and jumped out of the way. Drew looked over where the earth split open. He saw a floating egg-like rock floating in his gym. "What is this?" he asked himself as he looked at the rock.

"This is the power of earth, Drew." A female voice said. "You have been chosen to become my champion of earth."

Drew looks around, "Whose there? Where are you?" he said curiously.

"I am Gaia, and I am here to give you the power of the earth. So that you can use its ability." She said. "Gaia, huh?" Drew said. "So, stopped must I do to receive this so-called power?"

"Grab the rock and break it in half," Gaia replied. "And you will receive its power."

Drew followed the instructions as his skin got dry. "What's is happening?" he asked as his skin started turning into rock. "Relax, this will only take a minute," Gaia said. Soon the transformation completed, "You are now, The

Azure of Earth," Gaia stated. "There are two other Azure's roaming around. Fire and Water are looking for someone like you."

"Find them, team up, and stop whoever needs to be stopped. Got it." Drew confirmed.

"Right. I now dub you, Rocky, The Azure of Earth." Gaia declared. "Now go and meet the others."

"Got it," Rocky replied as he headed out to find Magma and Kira. Magma looked around, "That felt weird." Magma proclaimed, "Was that an earthquake just now?"

"I don't know. It happened so suddenly," Kira replied. "Was it another Azure?"

"Only one way to find out." Magma said as they started running to where the earthquake originated. "Do you think we'll find another Azure, Kira?" Magma asked. "Hopefully," Kira replied.

Just then, Magma and Rocky collided with each other. "Magma, are you alright?" asked Kira.

"Yeah, I'm fine," Magma said as he got back up and looked at Rocky. "By the looks of it, we found the Azure of Earth." he continued as he helped Rocky back up.

"I am Kira, the Azure of water," Kira began. "And this

undead you bumped into is Magma, The Azure of fire. What is your name?"

"Rocky, Azure of Earth," he stated, "Gaia told to meet with you two."

Kira and Magma look at each other "Gaia?" They asked. "Anyway, shall we search if any more Azures are here?" Kira asked, "But where should we even start?" Rocky asked, "Would the next one be air?"

"Darkness looks like it," Magma stated. "How would you know?" Kira asked, looking at Magma. "There," Magma replied as he pointed at the dark cloud above them.

CHAPTER 4

As the trio tried to develop a plan on entering the dark cloud, on the inside, a young female with short black hair with light blue highlights by the name Princess Cosmos was wandering around. "Hello?" she called out. "Is anyone here? How did I get here?"

As she turned the corner, "Welcome, Princess," a voice said. She got nervous heard the voice. "Show yourself," She called out as she looked around.

"I have been waiting for this day to give you your powers, Princess." The voice continued, "And you have reached the age to receive your dark ability."

"Out of everyone, Why me? Why not anyone else?" Princess asked. He steps out from the shadows relieving himself as Dracula. "Because you are my daughter, dear Princess," he said.

Princess crosses her arms, "Still haven't answered my questions, father." she retorted. "Because you can control it, and its great power," he replied. "I know you have it within you ever since you were a wee lass,"

Princess sighs, "Fine," she said, agitated, "What will happen when I get these powers?"

"You will become the Azure of Darkness. You will learn as you go." Dracula replied. "Are there other of these Azures?" Princess asked.

Dracula looks at her. "Why yes, right now there are three," he started to say, "Fire, water, and earth, and their right below us." Princess looks at them, "Why do I get the feeling I met the fire one before?" she asked. "Are they the only ones?" Princess looked up at Dracula. "For as I know, yes," he responded. "Now, are you ready to receive your powers?"

She looked away, thinking about it. "How do I become this Azure of darkness? Will it hurt?" she asked. Dracula steps closer, placing two fingers on her head. "This will not hurt a bit," he stated as darkness arises covering Princess.

Princess soon woke up, finding herself in Magma's arms. "Where am I?" She asked as her tiny wings on her lower back fluttered. Magma looked down at her, "Oh good. You're awake," Magma said. "We saw you float down from the dark cloud unconsciously and decided to help."

Princess looks at Kira and Rocky. "May I ask what your names are?" she asked.

"I'm Kira, Azure of water," Kira replied happily. "This big guy is Rocky, Azure of earth, obviously, and the one carrying you is Magma."

"What's yours?" Rocky asked, looking at her, smiling. "My name is Princess, Princess cosmos," Princess said. "Oh, your royalty?" Magma asked. Princess looked at him, then down. "Not that I know of or remember," she said as she rubbed her head. "By the way, where are we going?"

"To an abandoned warehouse that we can use as our hideout and home that Rocky said he knows where it is." Magma stated. "Of course," Rocky said smiling, "Don't worry, we're almost there."

Rocky pointed. "See, it's right there," he said.

"It needs a few repairs and maybe some decorations, and it'll be home," Kira said.

"Let's look inside," Magma said as they went inside.

CHAPTER 5

As the Azures went inside the warehouse, five unknown figures got together a block away. "Hehe, Hahaha," The hyper one said, "Can we get them now? Come on, Let's get them."

"It'll be too easy and done too quickly. That's not the plan," the leader said. "The boss is right, Snarl. You must be patient," Bonecrusher said calmly. "The time has yet to come to fight them." As Snarl Calmed down, "Why must we wait?" Snarl growls, "Ever I lost my title to him all those years ago, I want to take back what's mine by defeating Stewie."

"Snarl be quiet!" the boss growled, "You will get your chance, I promise." The boss looked at the female gunslinger.

"I have a job for you, Bluestar," He said. She smiled and replied, "Yes, sir?"

"I want you to sneak into there and see what you can discover and report back," the boss said. "Yes, sir," Bluestar said as she started walking towards the warehouse.

Meanwhile, inside the warehouse, the Azures were organizing the boxes. "I'll be happy when this is done," Princess said. "What are we doing with these boxes again?" Magma said.

As he finished stacking some boxes, "We're making our rooms, Magma." Kira called out as she finished her section, "So we can have some privacy at the bare minimum."

After they finished, "Hey guy's" Princess called out, "You may want to take a look over here." The other walked towards her, "What's up, pri…" As he saw the humanoid-like creature in the large tube and computer next to it, Magma started to say.

Kira steps closer to it, "You guys think it's friendly?" She asked them as she looked at it. Just then, it opened its eyes and looked at Kira. "Kira, it's looking at you," Rocky said calmly.

"Why you must be the four Azure's." It spoke, "I… was wondering… when you four will come around." The four looked at it in wonder. "What do you mean you've been waiting for us?" Magma said, surprised as he got in a stance. The creature looked at Magma. "My, what a feisty one you are." The creature said, "Yes, I have been waiting for the first four Azures for some time."

"The what, now?" Kira asked. "The Hidden," the creature replied. "The Hidden is a group of elemental super soldiers."

"Then who turned them into these 'super soldiers'?" Magma asked. "Their boss did. He is the one who engineered them into the super soldiers giving them enhanced strength, speed, and unique elemental powers." The creature said, "How he did this, even I don't know."

Then he realized, "How rude of me, let me introduce myself. My name is Tehutti. I am an archaeologist and trainer for the elementals." He said, "May I get your names?"

"Well, I'm Magma," He said as he placed his hand on his chest. "This is Kira, the big guy back there is Rocky, and this one here is Princess."

"Nice to meet you all," Tehutti said. Bluestar was hiding out of sight listening to everything.

"Can one of you let me out? I would like to discuss the future of this team," Tehutti said. "Storytelling, right?"

Rocky asks as Magma presses a few buttons and opens Tehutti's tube. "In a way, yes, Rocky, so listen well," Tehutti replied.

"Oh, I'll listen, and I'll tell the rest too," Bluestar said.

CHAPTER 6

As Tehutti finished his story, Bluestar snuck out and got back to the others. "You were in there for a while, Bluestar," Bonecrusher said. Bluestar looks at him "Aww, someone was worried about me." she said, smiling. "Just didn't want you to get hurt Bluestar," he said smiling. "Love you too, Bonecrusher," Bluestar replied as she walked up to him and kissed him. "What was the reason you were in there for so long, Bluestar?" Snarl asked.

"They found him," she replied. "I was waiting in there to see what they would do. Tehutti decided to become their mentor."

"Did you learn anything else while you were in there, Bluestar?" The boss asked. "They know about us, sir," Bluestar replied. Meanwhile, inside, "We should train our powers," Kira said. "Where are we gonna do that, Kira?" asked Rocky.

"I have a training room for you four." Tehutti contributed. The four of them looked at Tehutti, "Where?" Magma asked. Tehutti walks to a specific wall and pushes a panel making the border open, showing a large room. "Right here," Tehutti said. "Wouldn't we end up destroying the place Tehutti?" Princess asked worriedly. Tehutti smiled and looked at Princess, "Worry not young one," he said, "This section can handle your guy's intense powers."

As they started walking into the room, Princess stopped. "Are you sure the room will handle the abuse from our powers?" She asked. "Trust me," Tehutti said smiling, "No need to worry about it coming down."

"So, who'll go first?" Rocky asked. Tehutti walks in, "The training will start shortly," He started saying, "True power comes from your heart and instinct, and soon you will unlock your beast forms."

"Our what now?" Rocky asked.

Tehutti turned and looked at Rocky. "The Azure's have more than one form, and each of you has a unique beast form," he said.

"How will we get them, Tehutti?" Kira asked. "Only time will tell, Kira. Only time will tell," Tehutti replied.

"It feels like you do know more than your letting on Tehutti." Magma said. "Magma, my dear boy, over time, you will know everything" Tehutti said, "Now, let us train."

CHAPTER 7

As the Azures train with Tehutti in the training room, the Hidden were arguing outside the warehouse. "We should go in there and just defeat them!" Snarl growled.

"And I'm telling you snarl," the last hidden said, "We should wait and let them come to us."

"Why should we wait?" Snarl yelled. "You guys know if we wait on them, they are just going to defeat us, right?"

"What is the real reason you want to fight Snarl?" The boss questioned, "Why do you feed this hatred for magma?"

Snarl suddenly got pale and lowered his head, "There's a reason he won, and it's not that he excels in fighting." The others look at him, confused, "What do you mean, Snarl?" Bluestar asked as she walked to him.

"Magma," Snarl said as he looked up at them, "He is more than human."

"What do you mean, Snarl?" Bonecrusher asked.

Meanwhile, in the training room, "Again," Tehutti said as Magma hops back up and gets in a fighting stance.

If you can't conquer yourself, how can you beat your opponents" Tehutti said as Magma said, "Wielding a sword without fear of it, Is to be unworthy of the blade."

Kira smiles and says, "He's just not a hundred percent used to the sword, but he knows how to fight. Just then, Magma sticks his sword into the ground as the clone rushes at Magma. "What is he doing?" Tehutti said. Magma dodges the clone's swipe and punches with both hands sending the clone through the wall as it catches on fire.

The others were shocked and looked at him. Magma pulls his sword out and puts it in his back scabbard.

"Perfect," Tehutti said. "Your element has two versions of power. Fire can be calming and also very dangerous."

"What next then?" Magma asked. Tehutti points to another room, "Your next training session."

Tehutti watched as Magma went into the next room. "That boy has something more to him than meets the eye," he said.

"Yeah, no kidding." Princess replied, "Good thing he's on our side."

Rocky and Kira both looked through the one-sided mirror, watching magma getting creative with his power. "Even now, he has that passion for getting creative for a battle," Rocky said. "I think this new power just gave him more inspiration," Kira said. "We better work on our power too."

Outside of the warehouse, "That's the story," Snarl said. "Wow, so we have something much more than a simple fire elemental," Bluestar said. "So that's why you needed the power so you can be his rival?" the boss asked. Snarl looked at him. "And to prove I can be just as strong as him."

CHAPTER 8

As the Hidden talked on, night fell. "Ok, Azures," Tehutti called, "Time to get some rest." Magma, currently practicing in the third room, didn't hear Tehutti. "Right," said the others.

"Magma, give it a break," Tehutti called out, and Magma kept ongoing. Rocky and Princess both sighed. "When will he learn to take a break?" Rocky asked. "Don't worry," Kira said, smiling, "I'll get him." As she walked into the room where Magma was in.

"Magma," she said, "Where are you?" she realized that what they saw was an illusion and found a note on the wall.

"If he is done, then where-" an unusual noise cut off her sentence. "Hello?" she asked. Then she saw something on the wall."

"Already way ahead of you, signed Magma," Kira read.

"How did he-?" she went to Magma's bedroom and saw him passed out.

Kira giggles. "I guess that he got tired and went to bed without saying anything," she said, smiling. "I will tell him tomorrow what I want to tell him." Princess appeared next to Kira. "You find him?" she asked.

"Sleeping," Kira replied.

"We should get some sleep, too," Princess said as they went to their rooms. Tehutti went around, making sure they were asleep. As he got to Magma's room, "wait for a sec," he said as he got to Magma's bed and took off the blanket.

"He is a sneaky one, ain't he?" Tehutti said, "Is he still training?"

Just then, Magma's head came rolling in. "Nope," he said, "I'm right here, Tehutti."

"What happened, Magma?" He asked.

Magma chuckled and said, "Must have slept wrong, I guess."

"Need help, Magma?" Tehutti asked as Magma's head hop onto the bed. "I think I got it," he said.

"By the way, Magma, I believe Kira has a message for you," Tehutti said.

"Really?" Magma asked. "I'll ask her tomorrow. I know she sang for me a couple of times at the boxing championships. What was the song again? I'll think of it later. For now, let's get some sleep." After they said their nights, Magma got up, took off his armor except for his left gauntlet, and laid back down.

"So, Kira has something to tell me?" Magma thought to himself. "I'll have to ask her tomorrow and see what's up then."

He notices Princess going to the roof, "What is she up to?" he said. "I should check on her." He soon opened the hatch leading to the top, lifted his head, and saw Princess sitting down with her head on her arms and knees. "You okay, Princess?" Magma asked.

Princess lifted her head and looked at him, "Yeah, yeah, I'm fine," She said.

Magma climbed onto the roof and sat down next to her. "Something is up to Princess, want to talk about it?"

he said. Princess put her head on his shoulder. "Can you stay here with me?" she asked. Magma looked at her "Sure, Princess," he said as he put his arm behind her holding her as they sat on the roof, looking up at the stars.

CHAPTER 9

As night fell and morning rose, "Where's magma?" Kira asked. "I think he's still on the roof," Princess replied. Just then, Magma's body walked into the room. "Will a headless Magma do, Kira?" Rocky joked. Magma's body turned to Kira and walked towards her.

"Okay, we need to find his head, everyone," Kira said. "Someone's in love," Princess joked. Kira turned red from blushing. "Do you love him, Kira?" Tehutti asked. As Kira turned a bright red and was about to reply, Magma's body crashed into some crates. They all looked over at him. "I'll get him," Princess said as she went over to him.

"I wonder how nothing catches fire when his armor touches something?" Rocky asked. "It's because he can control his heat," Tehutti said, "Although how high he can go is a mystery to me."

"Anyone else thinks his head is closer than we think?" Kira asked. As they looked around, Tehutti climbed to the roof and saw Magma sleeping. "Which one is the real one?" he asked himself as he walked closer to Magma. As he got closer, Magma disappeared. "It was an illusion?" Tehutti said, surprised. Rocky climbed up. "Hey Tehutti, we found him." He said.

Tehutti looked back at Rocky, "Where was he, Rocky?" Tehutti replied.

"He was hiding in his room and said he was testing us," Rocky said.

"Testing?" Tehutti questioned. "He and Princess thought of the idea last night and wanted to test it to see how well it worked," Rocky said as they walked down to the ground floor.

The others were waiting, "So, your powers are growing, Magma." Tehutti asked.

Magma looked at him, "Or I'm getting better at using what powers I'm giving." he replied sarcastically. Kira swung down, hitting his head, and said, "You made us worry about you."

"Magma, those illusions you made seem all too real,"

Tehutti said. Magma looked at him and replied, "That's the point with that. I'm thinking with that ability, and I could find out all I need to learn about my opponent."

"That's smart. With heat can come illusions," Rocky said. "It can prove useful with combating in most fights."

"I wonder if we could do something similar with our powers," Kira said.

As the day went on, Princess was in the training room, practicing her powers. "She's been in there for a good amount of time," Rocky said. "Should one of us go in there?"

Magma steps past him, "I say leave her. Princess needs the extra boost." he said.

"What needs the extra boost?" Princess asked as she stepped out of the room." Nice cue Princess," Kira replied. Princess looked at Kira. "What do you mean?" she asked. Kira and Rocky laugh as Princess looks at Magma.

CHAPTER 10

As the Azures talked, the Hidden waited outside. "When I give the signal, I want you four to separate and defeat them." the leader said. "Snarl, take Magma, Bluestar takes Kira, Bonecrusher takes Rocky, and Kurogane, you take Princess."

All four of them looked at their boss, "yes, sir," They said in unison.

The boss points to the building with an open hand as the four rush towards It gearing for a fight. "We shall see which side is superior, Tehutti," he said.

As the Azures talked and laughed, Tehutti sensed the Hidden approaching, "So they choose to attack now, huh?" he said to himself. He looked to the four.

"Prepare for your taste of battle, you four," Tehutti called out. The four looked at Tehutti and nodded. "About time too," Magma growled, "I was itching for a real fight," He said as he summoned his sword.

"You four take them out to your element as best you can and beat them there," Tehutti said, "you'll have an advantage then."

The doors burst open, and Snarl walks in first "Hello magma, You miss me?" he said. Magma growls, "It's been a while since we last fought," Snarl continued.

"You're wasting your breath, Snarl," Magma said. "Let's cut to the fight." Magma lunged toward snarl, pushing him back with a swing, and followed after with high velocity.

As the other started their fight, The Hidden's boss walked in. "Long time no see Fang," Tehutti said, "Yes, it has," Fang said. "20 long years, and you just now got your crew."

As they talked to each other, the battles waged on.

Magma fought Snarl, pushing him back to MT. Beatle, Kira, and Bluestar brought their fight to the beach, Princess and Kurogume took their fight to the shadows, and Rocky and Bonecrusher took their fight to a small rocky cliff.

"The reason I'm here is to finish what I started tehutti," Fang snarled.

"Why do you champion hatred, Fang," Tehutti said, "why nurse these sins of old?"

As Magma and Snarl crossed swords, "So Magma, you excelled at swordplay, I wonder how long you last?" said Snarl as they continued to clash swords."

In the meantime, at the beach battle, people started watching the fight between Kira and Bluestar. At the action of the shadows raged on in town. "What's wrong, little one? Kurogane said. "Are you afraid?" As he looked through the shadows, a giant shadowy claw came up behind him.

Chapter 11

As the battle with Rocky and Bonecrusher rages. "I must find a way to stop him," Rocky said, panting. Bonecrusher smiled and ran towards Rock. y "I'll make this quick," he said as he knocked him up into the air. Rocky came back down, crashing into the ground. "To live is to face one dilemma after another. The ones who survive are the ones who come up with answers in this sea of adversity." Bonecrusher said as Rocky got up. "It's only logical, therefore, that we all strive to prose as many answers as possible.

I'm I wrong?"

Rocky dusts himself off, and replies "You just gonna stand there and monologue at me?" Bonecrusher smiled as they launched at each other, catching each other. "So you're the supposed strong one of the Hidden," Rocky said. "What if I am, huh?" Bonecrusher replied. Rocky grins as he lifts Bonecrusher, leans back, smashing him in the ground, flips over him, and does it two more times with a more substantial impact causing the surrounded mountains to break. Bonecrusher gets up, cracking his neck. "I felt that one big guy," he said. "It's a shame no one told you how to unlock your beast forms, though, and it's the most effective way to beat us right now."

They continued to trade blows. As they fought, Bonecrusher smiled. "It's a shame, even with this new power, you couldn't protect your daughter," he said as he punched Rocky through several thick trees. "Mmph So-called strongest-" Bonecrusher started to say as a dark green light shot up into the sky. "What?" Bonecrusher said, surprised as multiple tiki-men circled the beam as a large foot stepped out of the green light. Tehutti felt the change of power. "So, one has found their way to unlock their beast power," he said. "Now, let us see how this fight ends."

The beam disappeared, revealing Rocky as a titan. "Well, ain't this something," he said as he looked at himself. Bonecrusher took a couple of steps back, looking up and Rocky's new form. "Even if you found a way to unlock your beast form, it's still not enough to beat me," he said as he charged at Rocky. As he gained speed, he jumped up and around Rocky. When Bonecrusher got to Rocky's arm, Rocky, with great speed, grabbed Bonecrusher and flung him across the field. As Bonecrusher bounces, making medium craters where he landed, Rocky followed after.

Bonecrusher picks himself up staggered, "Don't get cocky, man," Bonecrusher said as his hand went across his bottom lip. "This fight isn't over." As their fight continued, Tehutti smiled as he watched. "Good for now," he said. Fang looked at him, "Don't think this is over, tehutti." he said. "Even if your team wins, we'll be back even stronger."

As they continued their talk, Rocky and Bonecrusher continued fighting.

Bonecrusher gets slammed deep into the cliff hillside. "Stay calm, Rocky. You'll be done with this fight soon," he said. Bonecrusher explodes out of the hill and at Rocky. "This ends now!" Bonecrusher yelled as he raced towards Rocky. "I won't lose!"

Rocky raises his fist and slams it down upon Bonecrusher making a large explosion in the ground. Rocky lifted his hand, and Bonecrusher lay there defeated. Rocky reverts to his normal state and falls to his knees, panting.

"Well done, Rocky," Tehutti said, "Now let us let us see how the other three are doing."

CHAPTER 12

"Let's see how Kira is doing in her fight," Tehutti said. Kira and Bluestar continue their fight at the beach. Bluestar covered her shoulder. "She's pretty good at this shootout," she said as she healed her wound. Kira pointed her revolvers at Bluestar. "For someone like you, you could easily dodge my bullets," she said as she charged a shot. Bluestar quickly runs behind her. "Gotcha, girly," Bluestar said. Kira put the gun on her shoulder, "Funny. I was going to say the same thing." Kira said as she fired the shot hitting Bluestar knocking her back. "You have to be a lot more surprising than that, Bluestar," Kira called out. "It's funny how you can learn from people like Magma." she continued as she started to daze off.

Bluestar saw what Kira was doing and knocked Kira back with a cannon-like water ball.

'Oof," Kira grunted, "I gotta pay more attention."

"You were doing so well." Bluestar taunted. "I didn't ask for your opinion, Bluestar," Kira replied. "Plus, shouldn't you watch what's happening around you?"

"What do you mean?" Bluestar said. Kira smiles as she places her hands down on the ground and uses several water pillars to attack Bluestar before hitting her with a tidal wave. Bluestar gets back up, "Let's test these for real, shall we?" Bluestar said as she jumped into the ocean.

"Big mistake, Bluestar," Kira said as she jumped into the ocean after her.

"Let's see just how much better she is in the water," Tehutti said.

In the depths of the ocean, Bluestar and Kira moved much faster, sending shock waves through the entire sea. Soon after, Kira started getting a blue aura around her. Schools of fish, sharks, and other aquatic life circled Kira.

"What's going on?" Bluestar questioned.

After a minute, Kira had turned into a mermaid-like creature as she gained long bluish-green hair, a fin at the top of her head, a long green tail from behind, and greenish-blue skin.

Bluestar looked at Kira with an open mouth and wide eyes. "Whoa, a-amazing," she said. Kira looked over at Bluestar, "Now then, is it time to end this little charade?" Kira said as she sent her fish army after Bluestar.

Bluestar dashed around in the water, trying to avoid the fish and sharks as Kira appeared behind her and slashed her with her aqua sword sending Bluestar zooming through the water. Tehutti was amazed at how eloquent Kira was with her new form. "She's got control of her power just like Rocky," Tehutti said.

Kira caught up with Bluestar and smiled as she grabbed Bluestar and started spinning around at Mach two. "Here we go," Kira said as she launched Bluestar through the ocean and onto land with a piranha on her foot, unconscious.

Kira jumps out of the ocean and points to the sea. The piranha looks at her and hops back into the sea, and Kira heals Bluestar's wounds as she turns back into her standard form.

Tehutti smiled, "Two for two, Fang," He said as he looked at him. "Don't get ahead of yourself. There's still two more," Fang said.

CHAPTER 13

"Let's see how Princess is doing," Tehutti said. In-Town, the battle of the shadows continued. Kurogane walked around looking through the darkness for Princess. "I know you're here, Princess," he said. "What's wrong, too afraid to fight? To lose?"

Princess watched him, trying to come up with a plan to defeat him. She waves her hand, causing a large shadow to cover the block, making it easy for her to move around silently. Kurogane looks around. "You think this little trick will help you?" he said as he grabbed down and pulled up Princess by her throat. "Hello, love," he continued, "Did you miss me?"

"I don't think anyone would miss that ugly mug of yours," Princess replied sarcastically. "Oh. You're a quick one, huh?" Kurogane asked. "Knowing my history, I am much more than just a quick tongue," Princess said as the shadow formed into a giant hand. "Sometimes losing focus on your surroundings can be deadly."

The colossal shadow hand grabs Kurogane, slams him on the ground a few times, and launches him through a building. Princess thought to herself, "So the bigger the shadow I make, the stronger the attack,"

"It's a shame you won't be able to put it into action much," Kurogane said behind her as he launched her through a steel building. "You think you can just use your power that easily!" Just then, a shadow covers the entire city as Princess stands back up, hurt. She pulls a piece of steel out of her shoulder, grunting. "You may want to run, Kurogane," she said as she started heading towards him. "Ooh, I'm so scared," he said with confidence.

Princess starts getting a dark aura around her as the shadow begins shrinking. "What are you planning?" Kurogane asked. Princess continues to head towards him, gaining speed as her aura turns into a shadowy demon and crashes into Princess, transforming her. As the dust settles, day turns to night, Kurogane looks around. "What's happening? What are you doing?" He said.

Princess stands up, as she is now greyish skin with a blue tint around her, a dark Dancer costume.

Tehutti felt that Princess's aura excited expectations. "Her aura feels a lot heavier than the other two," he said with his eyes widened, "A present of a stronger vampire flows through her."

Princess covers the city in darkness, "No more buildings should be destroyed," she said as she looked at Kurogane. "Are you ready?"

Kurogane gets mad and launches at Princess as she disappears. "Where are you?" Kurogane yelled. "Right behind you," Princess said as she raised and poked him, sending him several miles as he gets attacked along the way. Kurogane gets up, bruised and bloodied. "This isn't over!" he growled. Princess appears in front of him, biting his neck. "Now it is," she said as she took away his dark powers. Kurogane falls to his knees as Princess reverts to her normal state, and the darkness disappears.

"No way," Fang said. "She has that type of power?" Tehutti got worried, "Looks like we'll have to watch her closely." He replied.

CHAPTER 14

Tehutti turns his attention to the fiery battle that raged on at Mt. Beatle.

Swords clash at high speed, "Don't you ever think how you happen to be good at fighting even with little practice," Snarl said. "Just natural, I guess," Magma replied as he pushed snarl's sword away and slashed down his shirt.

Snarl growls and lunges at magma, clashing swords again. "This time, I will beat you," Snarl said. Just then, a Rapier Slashes Snarl's back. He turns around, seeing magma in a lava renaissance suit and gauntlets as Magma smiles. "The thing is you think just brute strength will be enough to be me," he said. "You never tried anything new, which is why you keep losing."

Snarl growls and lunges at Magma as he swiftly dodges and slashes at his back again. Snarl grunts and turns back.

"You know, I have this power to make authentic illusions and have it fight you, but knowing you, it'll be boring." Magma said. "So let's just do this," he grabbed his sword handle with both hands and pulled away, giving himself two identical swords. "This will be much more fun."

Magma launched at Snarl, slicing past him. Snarl blocks both swords but gets hit with a third strike. "What? How?" Snarl question. Magma looked over his shoulder and said, "What I like to call my two swords., three sword strike."

Magma turned to Snarl and asked, "Are you afraid? I know I am."

"Afraid of what? Your colossal amount of power, you're dreaming if you believe that Magma." Snarl said.

Magma laughed. "There's something I've been taught, not fearing my strength and the strength of my opponents, makes you no man at all," he said as he remembers what an old friend told Him. As they continued to fight, the earth started to rumble. Tehutti looked around. "No, it can't be." He said, "Magma is your power growing beyond your control?"

Mt. Beatle started leaking lava with a clash of swords, with sirens started alerting the nearby towns. As they continued to fight, an unchecked power began to grow in Magma. "This power, it's growing," Magma said as his attacks got stronger as he sent Snarl back through the base of Mt. Beatle.

Snarl jumps back to where Magma is, "Wanna see why they call me Hothead?" Magma said with a twitch. "Magma, let's not," Snarl said, stepping back. Magma turned his head to Snarl and appeared in front of him, uppercutting him to the top of the volcano.

As Snarl gets up, Magma is already there looking different as his lava armor starts getting thinner. "What's happening to you, Magma?" Snarl asked. Magma grows a long tail with a double-bladed battle-ax at the tip. The lava covers his face making it look demonic with a blade on either side of his face and top of his head and claws on his hands and feet. Snarl takes a couple of steps back, "What are you?" he asked.

Small yellow flames light his eyes as he looks at Snarl. Magma howls, sending a shockwave through Hawaii sending Snarl back. The Volcano explodes with intensity as Magma races towards Snarl.

"No, This can't be," Tehutti exclaimed.

Magma slashed at Snarl as he tried to block. Magma sends Snarl through the volcano again, getting burned on his shoulder by the lava. Magma roars again. Just then, a helicopter flies down, and Bluestar opens the door reaching her hand towards Snarl. "Grab on!" she yelled. The hurt Snarl reaches up, grabbing her hand, and Bluestar pulls him in. Magma runs after them and jumps on the helicopter, holding Snarls legs. "GO, GO, GO" Bluestar yelled as they lifted and shook Magma off, sending him into the erupting volcano.

CHAPTER 15

Several hours later, after the lava had stopped just as it reached the border of the towns. The remaining Azures got back together happily. Princess looks around, "Wait, where's Magma?" she said worryingly. The other two looked around, "Yeah, shouldn't he be around too?" Rocky asked.

"Maybe he's at the beach. He did say that the water calms him down," Kira said.

All three of them looked around at the beach, trying to find him. "Any luck?" Rocky asked. Both Kira and Princess shook their heads. Tehutti came to the beach, "So you three had the same idea?" He said. "He may have gone into the volcano to stop the flow." Just then, the earth started shaking. "What again?" Kira asked. The volcano began to break. "What's going on there?" Princess asked.

As the volcano breaks down, a giant crimson dragon

soars into the sky. "Is that?" Rocky stated. "Yes, That is Magma," Tehutti said. "The same presence is the same as our Magma."

But where is he going?" Princess asked. "Perhaps wherever he needs to go, maybe he is doing it subconsciously, going to find someone who can help him control that immense power," Tehutti replied. "I just hope Magma can find whoever can help him and come back soon," Princess said, saddened as her eyes started to water.

Kira wraps her arm around Princess, "I'm sure we will be back, Princess, and he'll be even better. You'll see," she replied. "No need to be sad, plus when he does come back, I'm sure you and he have lots to talk about."

Princess wiped her eyes, "I'll show him. I'll get stronger for him." she said. Rocky put his hands on their shoulders, "We'll all get stronger for him." Rocky said as a roar can be heard from Magma for miles like it was Magma calling out, "I'll get better for you guys!"

Tehutti smiled. "We'll be waiting for you, Magma."

CPSIA information can be obtained
at www.ICGtesting.com
Printed in the USA
BVHW030447281221
624883BV00009B/346/J